Star Light,
Star Bright

Hello and
Good-bye

Where
the Clouds
Go

HBJ HARCOURT BRACE JOVANOVICH, PUBLISHERS
Orlando   San Diego   Chicago   Dallas

Hello and Good-bye

ODYSSEY An HBJ Literature Program
Second Edition

Sam Leaton Sebesta

Consultants

Elaine M. Aoki   Myra Cohn Livingston

Willard E. Bill   Daphne P. Muse

Sonya Blackman   Sandra McCandless Simons

Sylvia Engdahl   Barre Toelken

Acknowledgments

For permission to reprint copyrighted material, grateful acknowledgment is made to the following sources:

William Cole: "Do You Know the Man?" by Shel Silverstein from *Oh, How Silly,* edited by William Cole. Copyright 1970 by Shel Silverstein.

William Collins + World Publishing Co., Inc.: "Gee lee, gu lu, turn the cake" from *Chinese Mother Goose Rhymes* by Robert & Lee Wyndham. Copyright © 1968 by Robert & Lee Wyndham.

The Dial Press: A Boy, a Dog, and a Frog by Mercer Mayer. Copyright © 1967 by Mercer Mayer.

Doubleday & Company, Inc.: "The Chair" by Theodore Roethke from *The Collected Poems of Theodore Roethke.* Copyright 1950 by Theodore Roethke.

E. P. Dutton: "Happiness" from *When We Were Very Young* by A. A. Milne. Copyright 1924 by E. P. Dutton; renewed 1952 by A. A. Milne.

Four Winds Press, a division of Scholastic Magazines, Inc.: "Hopscotch" from *The Hodgepodge Book,* collected by Duncan Emrich. Text copyright © 1972 by Duncan Emrich. "Four legs up and four legs down" from *The Nonsense Book* by Duncan Emrich. Text copyright © 1970 by Duncan Emrich.

Harcourt Brace Jovanovich, Inc.: "An old silent pond" by Basho from *Cricket Songs: Japanese Haiku,* translated by Harry Behn. © 1964 by Harry Behn. "Understanding" from *The Moon and a Star* by Myra Cohn Livingston. © 1965 by Myra Cohn Livingston.

Harper & Row, Publishers, Inc.: Text from "Some people I know" in *Only the Moon and Me* by Richard J. Margolis (J. B. Lippincott Co.). Copyright © 1969 by Richard J. Margolis.

Holt, Rinehart and Winston, Publishers: "One, two, three, a-lary" from *A Rocket in My Pocket,* compiled by Carl Withers. Copyright 1948 by Carl Withers. Copyright © 1976 by Samuel H. Halperin.

Houghton Mifflin Company and The Macmillan Company of Canada Limited: "Skyscraper" from *Alligator Pie* by Dennis Lee. Copyright © 1974 by Dennis Lee.

Hal Leonard Publishing Corporation: "Barnyard Song" from *Songs to Grow On,* edited by Beatrice Landeck. Copyright © by Edward B. Marks Company.

Little, Brown and Company: "Bananas and Cream" from *One at a Time* by David McCord. Copyright © 1962 by David McCord. "Higglety, pigglety, pop!" from *Grandfa' Grig Had a Pig,* compiled and illustrated by Wallace Tripp.

Macmillan Publishing Company: "Mix a pancake" from *Sing-Song* by Christina Rossetti. Macmillan Publishing Co., Inc. 1924. *The Chick and the Duckling* by Mirra Ginsburg, illustrated by Jose Aruego. Copyright © 1972 by Mirra Ginsburg. Illustration © by Jose Aruego. *Changes, Changes* by Pat Hutchins. Copyright © 1971 by Pat Hutchins.

Margit W. MacRae: "Uno, dos, tres, cho—" from *Teaching Spanish in the Grades* by Margit W. MacRae. Published by Houghton Mifflin Company, 1957.

National Textbook Company: "Que es aquello" and "What is it that stands?" from *Mother Goose on the Rio Grande* by Frances Alexander. Copyright © 1973 by National Textbook Company.

Oxford University Press: "One, two, three, four, five" from *The Oxford Dictionary of Nursery Rhymes,* edited by Iona and Peter Opie. Published by the Oxford University Press, 1951.

G. P. Putnam's Sons: "After Supper" from *Here, There, and Everywhere* by Dorothy Aldis. Copyright 1927, 1928 by Dorothy Aldis.

Random House, Inc.: "Green cheese, yellow laces" from *The Mother Goose Book* by Alice and Martin Provensen. Copyright © 1976 by Alice and Martin Provensen.

Russell & Volkening, Inc., as agents for the author: "Hello and Good-bye" by Mary Ann Hoberman. Copyright © 1959 by Mary Ann Hoberman.

Schroder Music Company (ASCAP): From the song "I Live in a City," words and music by Malvina Reynolds. Copyright 1961 by Schroder Music Co. (ASCAP). All rights reserved.

Western Publishing Company, Inc.: "The Gingerbread Boy," adapted from *The Tall Book of Nursery Tales.* Copyright © 1944 by Western Publishing Company, Inc.

Art Acknowledgments

Tom Dunnington: 75, 81; Jack Wallen: 109, 135 bottom, 137 top, 159, 160.

Cover: Tom Leonard

Contents

To Market, to Market   A Mother Goose rhyme   *8*

Green Cheese, Yellow Laces   An old rhyme   *10*

Mix a Pancake   A poem by Christina Rossetti   *12*

Bananas and Cream

From a poem by David McCord   *14*

CONNECTIONS: **Eating Healthful Foods**

(Health)   *16*

Uno, Dos, Tres, Cho–

A Mexican counting rhyme   *22*

One, Two, Three, Four, Five

An old counting rhyme   *24*

A Boy, a Dog, and a Frog

A story in pictures by Mercer Mayer   *28*

An old silent pond   A haiku by Basho   *35*

The Three Bears

An English folk tale retold in pictures   *36*

LEARN ABOUT STORIES:

Story Places, Story Faces *50*

The Chair A poem by Theodore Roethke *52*

Some People I Know

A poem by Richard J. Margolis *53*

After Supper A poem by Dorothy Aldis *54*

The Chick and the Duckling

From a story by Vladimir Suteyev *56*

CONNECTIONS: **Baby Animals** (Science) *76*

Barnyard Song A Kentucky folk song *82*

LEARN ABOUT THE LIBRARY:

Rabbit Gets a Library Book *88*

I Live in a City From a song by Malvina Reynolds *92*

Skyscraper A poem by Dennis Lee *94*

Changes, Changes

A story in pictures by Pat Hutchins *96*

One, Two, Three, A-lary A rhyme *110*

Hopscotch A rhyme *112*

Gee Lee, Gu Lu An old Chinese rhyme *113*

The Gingerbread Man

A play based on an American folk tale *114*

LEARN ABOUT STORIES: **Story Mix-Up** *136*

What Is It? Two riddles *138*

Hickory, Dickory, Dock

A Mother Goose rhyme *140*

Higglety, Pigglety, Pop An old rhyme *142*

Do You Know the Man?

A poem by Shel Silverstein *144*

Understanding

A poem by Myra Cohn Livingston *146*

Hello and Good-bye

A poem by Mary Ann Hoberman *147*

CONNECTIONS: **The Seasons**

(Social Studies) *150*

Happiness A poem by A. A. Milne *156*

KEY WORDS *157*

SOUNDS AND LETTERS *159*

To Market, To Market

A Mother Goose rhyme

To market, to market,
  To buy a fat pig,
Home again, home again,
  Jiggety-jig.
To market, to market,
  To buy a fat hog,
Home again, home again,
  Jiggety-jog.

Picture by Tony Kenyon

9

Green Cheese, Yellow Laces

An old rhyme

Green cheese,
Yellow laces,
Up and down
The market places.

Picture by Tony Kenyon

11

Mix a Pancake

A poem by Christina Rossetti

Mix a pancake,
Stir a pancake,
    Pop it in the pan;
Fry the pancake,
Toss the pancake,—
    Catch it if you can.

Pictures by Marie-Louise Gay

Bananas and Cream

From a poem by David McCord

Bananas and cream,
Bananas and cream,
All we could say was
Bananas and cream.

We couldn't say fruit,
We wouldn't say cow,
We didn't say sugar—
We don't say it now.

Picture by Sharon Harker

Bananas and cream,

Bananas and cream,

All we could shout was

BANANAS AND CREAM.

Eating Healthful Foods

MILK GROUP

Bix the clown says, "We need to eat foods from the milk group every day.

Drink some milk.

Eat some cheese.

What other foods from the milk group would you like to try?"

Pictures by Gwen Connelly

16

MEAT GROUP

Bix says, "We need to eat foods from the meat group every day."

Bix likes chicken, fish, and eggs.

He eats nuts and beans, too.

What kinds of food from the meat group do you like best?

BREAD AND CEREAL GROUP

Bix says, "Eat foods from the bread group every day.

Eat rice and noodles.

Try hot cereal and cold cereal.

Which foods from the bread group have you tried?"

FRUIT AND VEGETABLE GROUP

Bix says, "We need to eat foods from the fruit and vegetable group every day."

Bix eats apples and carrots.

He eats pears and corn.

Bix tries many kinds of fruits and vegetables.

19

EAT FOOD FROM FOUR FOOD GROUPS EVERY DAY.

You need foods from all four food groups every day.

They can help you stay healthy.

Bix the clown says, "Eat three good meals a day.

Eat foods that are good for you!"

Questions

A.   **B.**

C.   **D.**

1. Which foods are from the meat group?

2. Which foods are from the fruit and vegetable group?

3. Which foods are from the milk group?

4. Which foods are from the bread and cereal group?

Activity   Draw a Balanced Meal

On a piece of paper, draw a meal that you would like to eat.

Be sure it has foods from all four food groups.

Label the food groups.

Uno, Dos, Tres, Cho-

A Mexican counting rhyme

Uno, dos, tres, **cho-**

Uno, dos, tres, **co-**

Uno, dos, tres, **la-**

Uno, dos, tres, **te.**

Chocolate, chocolate,

¡bate, bate, el **chocolate!**

Picture by Sharon Harker

23

One, Two, Three, Four, Five

An old counting rhyme

One, two, three, four, five,

I caught a fish alive,

Pictures by Dennis Ziemienski

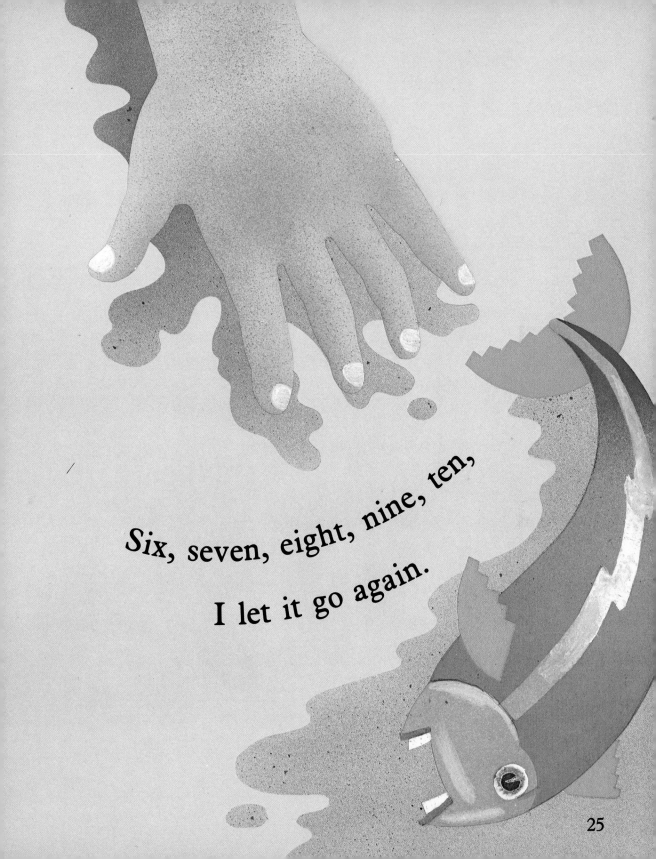

Six, seven, eight, nine, ten,

I let it go again.

Why did you let it go?
Because it bit my finger so.

Which finger did it bite?
This little finger on the right.

A BOY, A DOG, and A FROG

A picture story by Mercer Mayer

1

2

3

4

5

6

7

8

9

10

11

12

13

14

15

32

16

17

18

19

20

21

An old silent pond . . .
A frog jumps into the pond,
splash! Silence again.

A Japanese haiku by Basho

THE THREE BEARS

An English folk tale retold in pictures by Kinuko Craft

This porridge is too hot.

Let us go for a walk.
When we come back,
our porridge will be ready
to eat.

Somebody has been eating
my porridge—
and has eaten it all up!

43

Somebody has been sitting
in my chair—
and has sat the bottom out!

Somebody has been lying
in my bed—
and here she is!

Story Places, Story Faces

In each place along the road,
You'll find something wrong.
Tell who *should* be in each place
As you go along.

START

Grandma's House

Mr. McGregor's Garden

Little Boy Blue's Haystack

Little Miss Muffet's Tuffet

The Witch's Gingerbread House

Picture by Ed Taber

The Chair

A poem by Theodore Roethke

A funny thing about a Chair:

You hardly ever think it's *there*.

To know a Chair is really it,

You sometimes have to go and sit.

Picture by Roseanne Litzinger

Some People I Know

A poem by Richard J. Margolis

Some people I know
fill up the whole chair.
They don't share.

You don't share.

53

After Supper

A poem by Dorothy Aldis

Let's not pretend we're anywhere;
Let's only sit here in this chair.

I don't want to play that we
Are sailors sailing on the sea,
Or pirates in a pirates' cave
Or even lions being brave.

I'm feeling very nice and near.
Let's just be here.

Picture by Charles Robinson

The Chick
and the Duckling

A story by Vladimir Suteyev

Translated from the Russian by Mirra Ginsburg

Pictures by Jose and Ariane Aruego

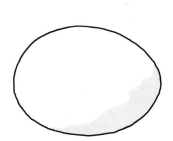

A Duckling came out
of the shell.
"I am out!" the Duckling said.

"Me too," said the Chick.

"I am taking a walk,"
said the Duckling.

"Me too,"
said the Chick.

"I am digging a hole,"
said the Duckling.

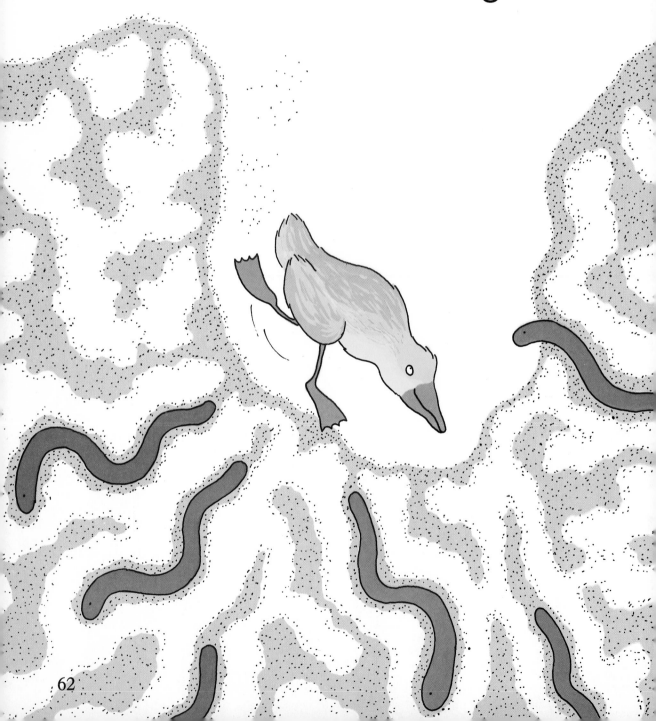

"Me too,"
said the Chick.

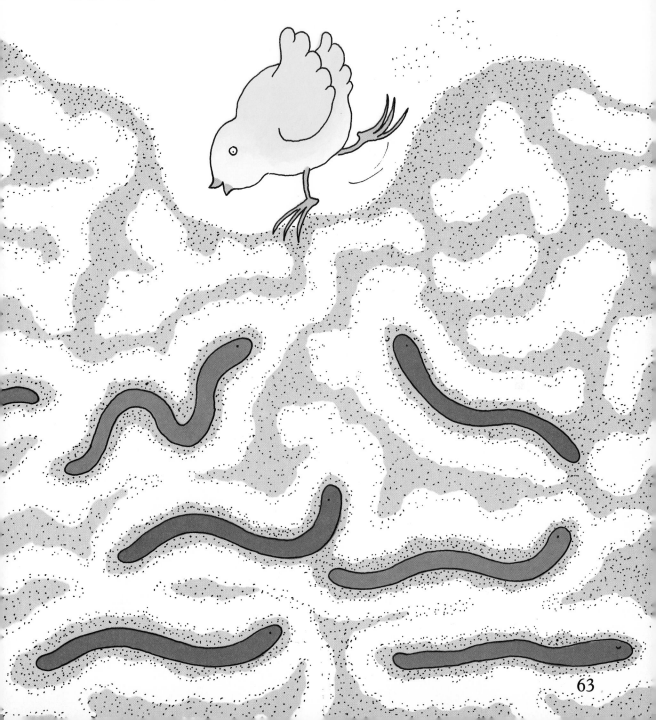

"I have found a worm,"
said the Duckling.

"Me too,"
said the Chick.

"I am swimming,"
said the Duckling.

"Me too!"
said the Chick.

67

The Duckling pulled
the Chick out.

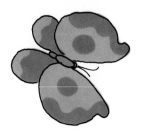

"I am going for another swim,"
said the Duckling.

"Not me,"
said the Chick.

Questions

A.  B.

1. Who can swim like me?

A.  B.

2. Who can dig like me?

A.  B.

3. Who can fly like me?

A.  B.

4. Who can run like me?

A.  B.

5. Who can get a worm like me?

Activity   I Can Do It Well

What can you do well at school?
Show what you can do well.

Baby Animals

Find the eggs.

Find blue eggs, white eggs,

brown eggs, and eggs with spots.

Some eggs are big.

Some eggs are tiny.

What will come out of the eggs?

Many animals lay eggs.

Do you see eggs in the water?

They are fish eggs.

Little fish grow inside of the eggs.

The little fish hatch out of the eggs.

Little turtles hatch.

Little birds hatch.

The baby animals are here!

What other baby animals can you find?

Some animals do not lay eggs.
The little animals grow inside
their mothers.
The little animals grow and grow.
Then the baby animals are born.

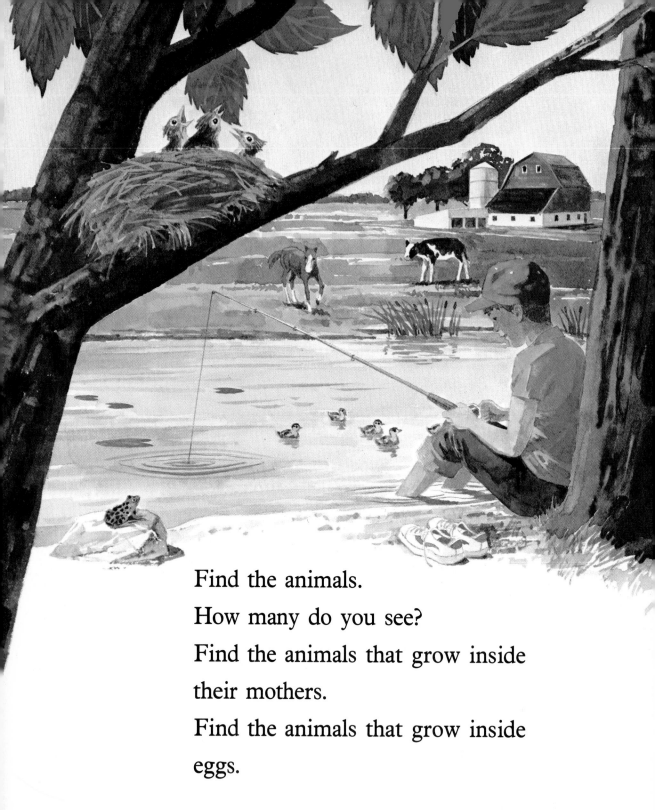

Find the animals.

How many do you see?

Find the animals that grow inside their mothers.

Find the animals that grow inside eggs.

Questions

Who is my mother?

Find a mother for each animal.

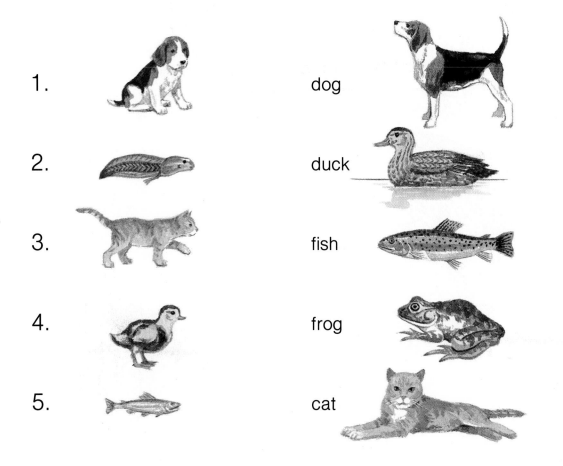

1.   dog

2.   duck

3.   fish

4.   frog

5.   cat

Activity   **Finish the Egg Story**

What will happen next?

Draw a picture.

Barnyard Song

A Kentucky folk song

I had a cat, and the cat pleased me,

I fed my cat under yonder tree.

Cat goes fiddle dee dee.

Pictures by Marie-Louise Gay

I had a hen, and the hen pleased me,
I fed my hen under yonder tree.
Hen goes chimmy chuck, chimmy chuck,
Cat goes fiddle dee dee.

I had a duck, and the duck pleased me,
I fed my duck under yonder tree.
Duck goes quack, quack,
Hen goes chimmy chuck, chimmy chuck,
Cat goes fiddle dee dee.

I had a cow, and the cow pleased me,
I fed my cow under yonder tree.
Cow goes moo, moo,
Duck goes quack, quack,
Hen goes chimmy chuck, chimmy chuck,
Cat goes fiddle dee dee.

Rabbit Gets a Library Book

Pictures by Ed Taber

90

I Live in a City

A song by Malvina Reynolds

I live in a city,
Yes I do,
I live in a city,
Yes I do,
I live in a city,
Yes I do,
Made by human hands.

Picture by Ted Carr

Skyscraper

A poem by Dennis Lee

Skyscraper, skyscraper,
Scrape me some sky,
Tickle the sun
While the stars go by.

Tickle the stars
While the sun's climbing high,
Then skyscraper, skyscraper
Scrape me some sky.

Pictures by Charles Robinson

95

Changes, Changes

A story in pictures by Pat Hutchins

Questions

What will help?

1.
2.
3.

Activity   Draw the Changes

On a piece of paper, draw a picture to show how each one will change.

1.
2.

One, Two, Three, A-lary

A jump-rope rhyme

One, two, three, a-lary
My first name is Mary;
If you think it's necessary,
Find it in the dictionary.

Picture by Linda Boehm Weller

111

Hopscotch

A rhyme

Hopscotch, let us hop,
Hopscotch, let us stop,
Let us hop, then you stop,
Let us stop, then you hop,
Hopscotch, hopscotch,
Let   us   hop!

Picture by Linda Boehm Weller

Gee Lee, Gu Lu

An old Chinese rhyme

Gee lee, gu lu, turn the cake,
Add some oil, the better to bake.

Gee lee, gu lu, now it's done;
Give a piece to everyone.

The Gingerbread Man

A play adapted from the American folk tale

Pictures by Willi Baum

Characters

Storyteller 1	**Little Old Woman**	**Cow**
Storyteller 2	**Little Old Man**	**Bear**
Storyteller 3	**Gingerbread Man**	**Fox**

Storyteller 1: Once upon a time
a little old woman
and a little old man
lived in a little old house.
They were very happy,
but they had no children.
They wanted a child
of their own.

Storyteller 2: One day the little old woman
was making gingerbread.
She laughed and said,

Little Old Woman: I'll make us a son
out of gingerbread!

Storyteller 3: So she rolled out the dough,
and she cut out a man.
She gave him raisin eyes,
a raisin mouth,
and a coat with raisin buttons.
Then she popped him
into the oven.

Storyteller 1: Before long,
the little old woman looked
to see if the gingerbread man
was done.

Storyteller 2: As soon as the oven door
was opened,
out he jumped!
Off he ran,
out the door,
and down the road.

Little Old Woman: Come back! Come back!

Storyteller 3: Called the little old woman.

Little Old Man: Come back! Come back!

Storyteller 1: Called the little old man.

Storyteller 2: But the gingerbread man
only laughed and said,

Gingerbread Man: Run, run, as fast as you can.
You can't catch me!
I'm the gingerbread man!

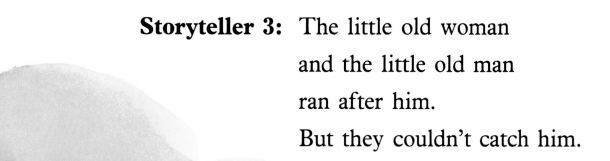

Storyteller 3: The little old woman
and the little old man
ran after him.
But they couldn't catch him.

Storyteller 1: A cow looked up
as the gingerbread man
ran by.
She called,

Cow: Come back! Come back!

Storyteller 2: But the gingerbread man
only laughed and said,

Gingerbread Man: Run, run, as fast as you can.
You can't catch me!
I'm the gingerbread man!
I've run away
From a little old woman,
And a little old man,
And I can run away
From you, too.
I can, I can!

Storyteller 3: The cow ran after
the gingerbread man.
But she couldn't catch him.

Storyteller 1: A bear was looking
for something to eat.
Just then,
the gingerbread man ran by.
The bear called,

Bear: Come back! Come back!

Storyteller 2: But the gingerbread man
only laughed and said,

Gingerbread Man: Run, run, as fast as you can.
You can't catch me!
I'm the gingerbread man!
I've run away
From a little old woman,
And a little old man,
And a cow.
And I can run away
From you, too.
I can, I can!

Storyteller 3: The bear ran after
the gingerbread man.
But he couldn't catch him.

Storyteller 1: Down by the river was a fox. Along ran the gingerbread man, saying,

Gingerbread Man: Run, run, as fast as you can.
You can't catch me!
I'm the gingerbread man!
I've run away
From a little old woman,
And a little old man,
And a cow,
And a bear.
And I can run away
From you, too.
I can, I can!

Storyteller 2: But the fox
did not run after him.
She just said sweetly,

Fox: I don't want to catch you,
gingerbread man.
But if you hop on my tail,
I will give you a ride
across the river.

Storyteller 3: The gingerbread man hopped
onto the fox's tail.
And they started
across the river.

Storyteller 1: When the water got deeper,
the fox called out,

Fox: Hop on my back
or you will get wet.

Storyteller 2: So the gingerbread man
hopped onto the fox's back.

Storyteller 3: When the water got deeper,
the fox called out,

Fox: Hop on my head
or you will get wet.

Storyteller 1: So the gingerbread man
hopped onto the fox's head.

Storyteller 2: Suddenly
the fox tossed back her head
and opened her mouth.

Storyteller 3: And that was the end
of the gingerbread man
and the end
of this story, too.

Questions

Bear

Fox

Cow

Gingerbread Man

Pig

Little Old Man
and Little Old Woman

1. Who ran after me first?

2. Who ran after me next?

3. Who ran after me then?

4. Who gave me a ride?

5. Who didn't get away from me?

swim   jump   walk   talk   run   laugh

6. What can I do?

7. What *can't* I do?

8. What would have helped me?

Activity   Write a New Story

The little old woman baked something new.

What did she bake?

What happened then?

Story Mix-up

In each story, you will see,

There is a mix-up

That you need to fix up.

Which pictures are 1, 2, and 3?

Pictures by Ed Taber

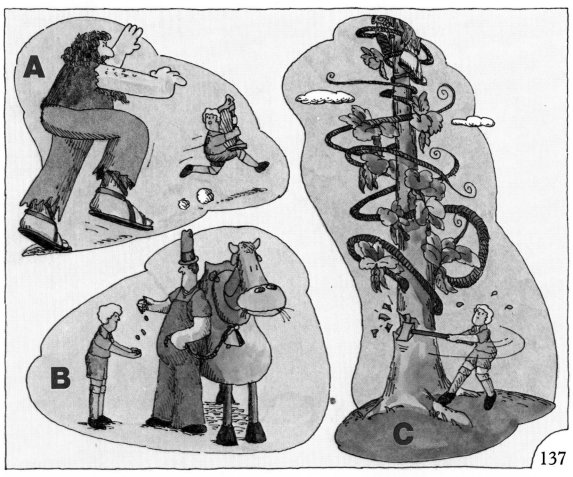

What Is It?

¿Qué es aquello
que colgado en la pared
da sin tener manos
y anda sin tener pies?

(El reloj.)

What is it that stands
  Or hangs on the wall,
Runs fast with its hands,
  Has no feet at all?

(A clock.)

—A Mexican riddle

Four legs up and four legs down,
Soft in the middle and hard all around.

(A bed.)

—An old American riddle

Hickory, Dickory, Dock

A Mother Goose Rhyme

Hickory, dickory, dock,

The mouse ran up the clock.

The clock struck one.

The mouse ran down,

Hickory, dickory, dock.

Picture by Sharon Harker

BONG

Higglety, Pigglety, Pop

An old rhyme

Pictures by Tony Kenyon

Higglety, pigglety, pop!

The dog has eaten the mop;

The pig's in a hurry,

The cat's in a flurry,

Higglety, pigglety, **POP!**

Do You Know the Man?

A poem by Shel Silverstein

Do you know the man with the flowers growing

Out of the top of his head?

Yellow flowers,

Purple flowers,

Orange, green, and red.

Growing there

Just like hair

Out of the top of his head.

(Yes, you heard just what I said—

Out of the top of his head.)

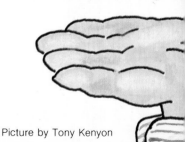

Picture by Tony Kenyon

Understanding

A poem by Myra Cohn Livingston

Sun
and rain
and wind
and storms
and thunder go together.

There has to be a little bit of each
to make the
weather.

Picture by Bob Baumgartner

Hello and Good-bye

A poem by Mary Ann Hoberman

Hello and good-bye
Hello and good-bye

When I'm in a swing
Swinging low and then high
Good-bye to the ground
Hello to the sky.

Hello to the rain
Good-bye to the sun,
Then hello again sun
When the rain is all done.

In blows the winter,
Away the birds fly.
Good-bye and hello
Hello and good-bye.

149

The Seasons

It is fall in my park.
It is getting cool.
Animals are getting ready for winter.

I like to watch the leaves turn
red and yellow.
They are coming down.
I like to play in the leaves with
my friend.

Pictures by Larry Mikec

It is winter in my park.
The trees have lost their leaves.
Soft snow is falling.
Does it snow where you live?

I put on my warm coat.
I like to play in the snow.

It is getting warm in my park.

It is spring.

Sometimes it rains.

Rain helps the plants grow.

Spring is my favorite season.

I like to look for birds' eggs.

I like to see baby animals

in the trees.

Summer is hot in my park.
Everything is growing.

I put on my shorts.
I like to play under the trees.
It is cooler here.
I play in the park all summer.
Then summer ends and a new
season begins again.

Questions

1. What happened in the park in the summer?

2. What happened in the park in the fall?

3. What happened in the park in the winter?

4. What happened in the park in the spring?

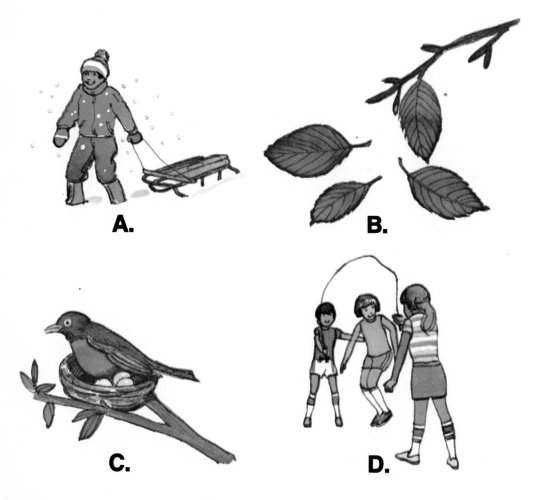

A.

B.

C.

D.

Activities

1. **Name Your Favorite Season**

   Write the name of your favorite season.

   Draw a picture that shows what you do in that season.

2. **Write About Trees and Seasons**

   On a piece of paper, write a sentence to tell what happens to the oak tree in each season.

In the fall, the oak

tree _____.

In the winter, the oak

tree _____.

In the spring, the oak

tree _____.

In the summer, the

oak tree _____.

Happiness

A poem by A. A. Milne

John had
Great Big
Waterproof
Boots on;
John had a
Great Big
Waterproof
Hat;
John had a
Great Big
Waterproof
Mackintosh—
And **that**
(Said John)
Is
That.

Picture by Stan Tusan

Key Words

**To Market,
To Market**

market   page 8

hog   page 8

**Green Cheese,
Yellow Laces**

lace   page 10

Mix a Pancake

pancake   page 12

fry   page 12

**Bananas
and Cream**

cream   page 14

**Eating Healthful
Foods**

meat   page 17

bread   page 18

cereal   page 18

fruit   page 19

vegetable   page 19

**Uno, Dos, Tres,
Cho-**

chocolate   page 22

**One, Two, Three,
Four, Five**

finger   page 27

**A Boy, a Dog,
and a Frog**

frog   page 28

**An Old Silent
Pond**

silence   page 35

The Three Bears

porridge   page 37

**Story Places,
Story Faces**

tuffet   page 51

haystack   page 51

gingerbread   page 51

The Chair

chair   page 52

**Some People
I Know**

share   page 53

After Supper

pretend   page 54

pirate   page 54

**The Chick and
the Duckling**

duckling   page 56

chick   page 56

shell   page 58

Baby Animals

hatch   page 78

Barnyard Song

pleased   page 82

yonder   page 82

Rabbit Gets a Library Book

library   page 88

I Live in a City

human   page 92

Skyscraper

skyscraper   page 94

Changes, Changes

change   page 96

One, Two, Three, A-lary

dictionary   page 110

Hopscotch

hopscotch   page 112

Gee Lee, Gu Lu

oil   page 113

The Gingerbread Man

dough   page 117

Story Mix-up

need   page 136

What Is It?

hand   page 138

feet   page 138

leg   page 139

middle   page 139

Hickory, Dickory, Dock

clock   page 140

Higglety, Pigglety, Pop

hurry   page 142

Do You Know the Man?

flower   page 144

Understanding

together   page 146

weather   page 146

Hello and Good-bye

swing   page 147

The Seasons

season   page 150

Happiness

waterproof   page 156

mackintosh   page 156

Sounds and Letters

/sk/

sky   page 94

/st/

star   page 95

/spl/

splash   page 35

/pl/

plant   page 152

/bl/

blue   page 76

/fl/

flower   page 144

/gr/

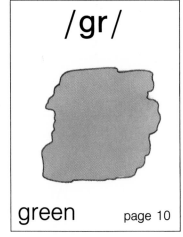

green   page 10

/br/

bread   page 18

/tr/

tree   page 82

/a/

cat

page 82

/a/

hatch

page 78

–and

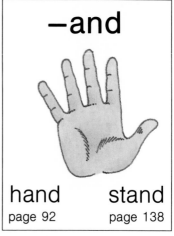

hand   stand

page 92   page 138

/i/

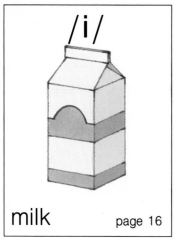

milk

page 16

/i/

fish

page 17

–it

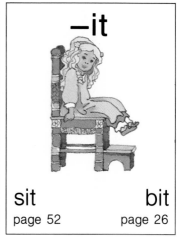

sit   bit

page 52   page 26

/u/

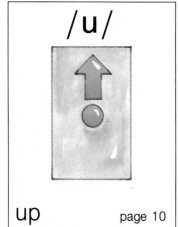

up

page 10

/u/

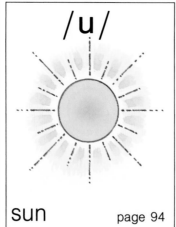

sun

page 94

–uck

duck   chuck

page 84   page 83

6 7 8 9 0 1 2 3 4 D E F G H I J